このシリーズの
名付け親です！！
はぴぱら
さつき

Satsuki Nao

FIRST PHOTO BOOK

小1400
大2500

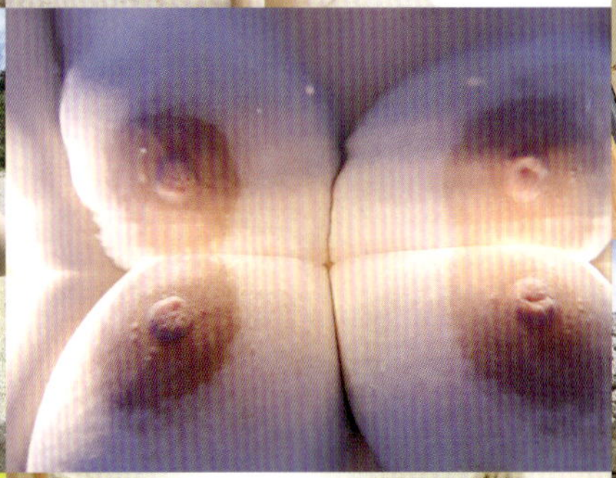

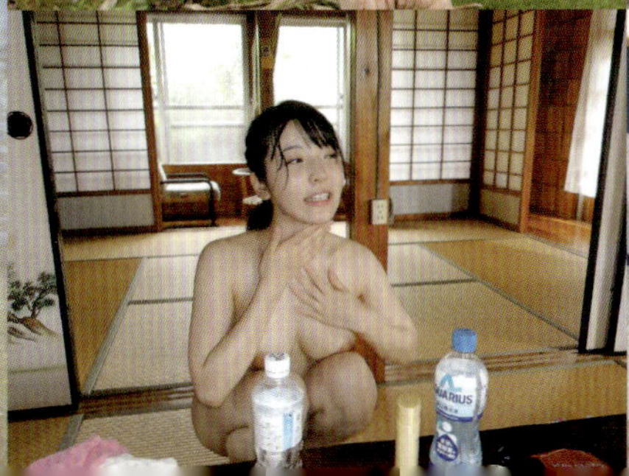

Essential

Courtyard

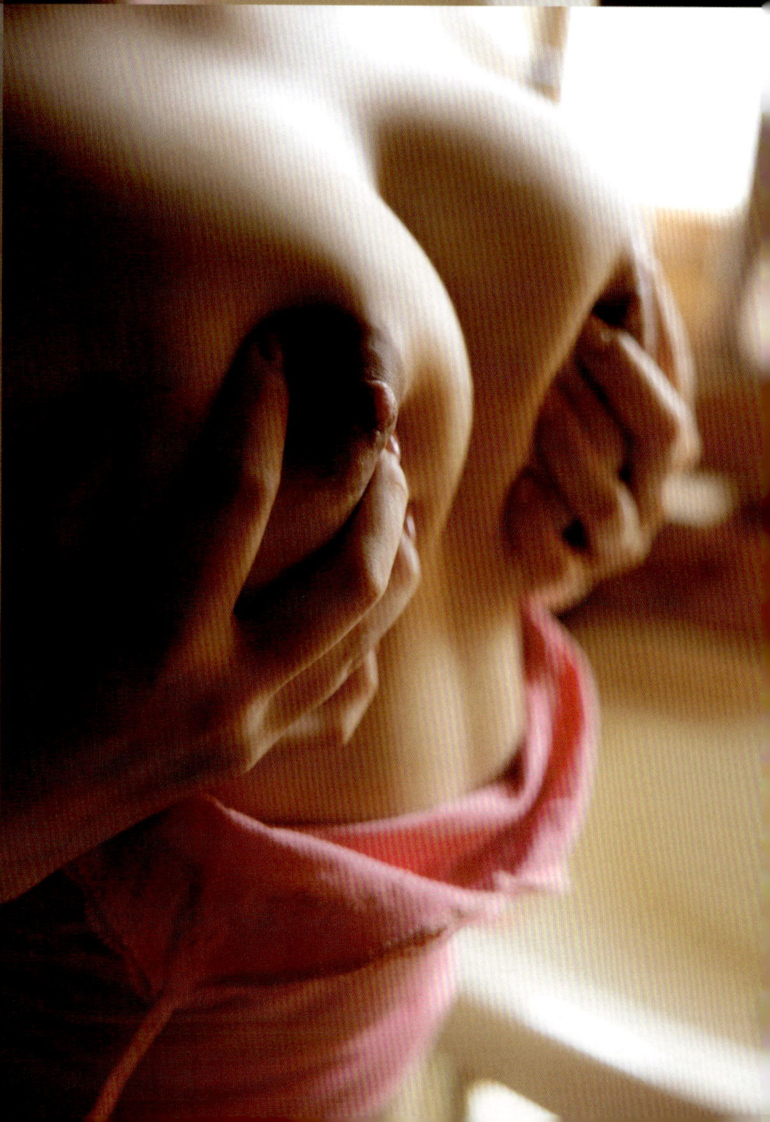

Satsuki Nao
FIRST PHOTO BOOK

Artist: SATSUKI NAO
Photographer: MAKIHARA SUSUMU
Styling & Hair and make-up: TOSHIKUNI ISAKO
Artist Management: SUGIMOTO TAKAMICHI (Bstar)
KAWAMATA HARUKA (Bstar)
Art Director: MIZUKI RYOTA
Editor: SHIBATA HIROSHI (TAKESHOBO)